it's just so... little!

written by Brenda Faatz & Peter Trimarco
illustrated by Peter Trimarco

Printed in the USA
Notable Kids Publishing • Colorado

Dedicated to
Chandler,
Tad &
Jon.

Early one morning
with sleep in her eyes,
Lizzy looked out the window
and to her surprise
her world had changed colors
while she was in bed.
Green leaves were now yellow,
orange and red.

She opened the door and was hit right away by the chilly fall air on this NOT so warm day.

It's just so...WINDy...

"It's time to go play! There's no time to lose!
Where is my jacket? I can't find my shoes!"

It's just so...MEGA MEasy.

She threw on her hoodie
and stared in surprise.
Her favorite jacket
was not quite her size.

It's just so.....PINCHY!

"It's ok," said her mother, "there's no need to frown.
Your hoodie will soon be a great hand-me-down."

"A great HAND-ME-WHAT?"
Lizzy asked of her mother.

"It's when we share clothes
with a sister or brother."

WHAT?!!!

"A sister? A brother? What does this mean?
Is it good? Is it bad? Or just soooo...in between?
Will I lose my room? Will you still play with me?
When will this happen? How Soon will it be?"

"The baby will be here in summer, my dear
after fall, after winter, and spring have been here.
I love you, my Lizzy, always and forever
and when baby comes, we will all play together."

Lizzy went out to play
but her tummy felt strange.
Her feelings were telling her
things would soon change.
As she soared on her swing,
thoughts swirling around,
Lizzy spied something small
down below on the ground.
When she looked closer,
what did she see?
There all alone,
a wee baby tree.

It's
just
so...

...little.

"It's getting so cold,
so snappy and chilly.
Will he be ok?
Will he? Oh, will he?

Inside where it's warm,
that's where he must go
before winter comes
and he's buried in snow."

"We can help, little one,"
Lizzy said with a smile.
"Come grow and get strong.
Stay with us for a while."

It's such a...
weeeeeeee sprout.

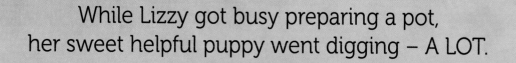

While Lizzy got busy preparing a pot,
her sweet helpful puppy went digging – A LOT.

It's just so...
...Dog-Diggity.

"You are drooping,"
she said to the wee baby sprout.
"Are you tired or sad?
OOOOH! Your water ran out."

It's just so...
...Droop-Dry-Drastic.

It's
just
so...

WETRAGEOUS!

Lizzy cared for the sapling,
her wee baby tree,
but as weeks went by
little change did she see.

It's just so...

...shhhhhhhh (it's sleeping).

Then early one morning
with sleep in her eyes
Lizzy woke and discovered
another surprise.
The first snow of winter
blew in like a twister.
WOWZA!
"I'm one season closer
to being a sister!"

It's just so......BLIZZARDY!

'Twas a white wonderland,
heaps of snow piling up
– time to build a snowman
with the help of her pup.
Lizzy searched for her gloves,
hat, scarf and snowsuit
and last but not least,
her shiny, red boots.

It's just a ... MESSA-RUCKUS!!

Oh Noooo!!
She called to her mother
with tears in her eyes,
"My boots got smaller.
They've shrunk half their size!"

It's just so...

...eek-ow-toe-tight!

"It's OK," said her mother.
"Your feet, they are growing.
The rest of you too –
your TALLER is showing.

We will get you new boots.
You will love them, you'll see...
and while we are at it,
some new pants for me."

They're just so...

...even better
...even REDDER.

It's just so...
Snowbomidable.

In from the cold
wet, chilly and frosty,
Lizzy drank her hot chocolate,
soooo marshmallow frothy!

It's just so...
chocolicious.

But the sapling was shaking
which made Lizzy worry.
"He must be cold too.
He needs help in a hurry!"

It's just so ...... sh-shake-a-ch-chilly.

Reading books about trees
and how to get warm,
soon a big, bright idea
took Lizzy by storm.

It's just so…………………

...Electra-dazzle-riffic!

"What's this? WHAT IS THIS??
It was not here before!
We should go to the doctor.
OH NO!
There are MORE!"

"Those are buds," father said,
"the beginning of leaves.
It is nature in Spring,
such magic it weaves."

It's just so......BUD-mazing!

Spring! It had sprung!
Splish-splashy rain showers!
Things changing like crazy
– trees bursting with flowers.

Lizzy looked all around
and saw something quite funny
– baby birds, baby ducks
and bunny after bunny.

It's just a......Bunnypalooza!!

They swam and played soccer,
with kites in the sky
and sat in the sun
–butterflies floating by.

It's just soooooooo........................

Spring flowed into Summer
days hotter and longer,
as Lizzy's wee tree
had grown fuller and stronger.

.......TREEMONDO-MONGOUS!

"MOM!!!!!...
My tree once soooo wee
has been growing and growing.
He's outgrown his pot!
His TALLER is showing!"

"It's OK," said her mother.
"This change has been coming.
Let's plant him outside
so his roots can keep running.
Then Mom needs your help
'cause you're growing up too.
Soon you'll be a big sister...
a job just for you."

It's just a little ....

.... BIG!

Lizzy planted her tree
with love and great care,
but knew she must hurry...
"There's no time to spare!"

To be a big sister
there's so much to do.
There's plotting and planning...

It's all just so.......new!

The day finally came.
"It's TODAY!
Make Way!
They are coming home NOW!
It's our baby's BIRTH day!"

"We've got diapers and bottles
and red boots," she cried.
"I'm excited! I'm scared!"
ALL THESE FEELINGS INSIDE!!!!

It's
just
so...

GIGANTONORMOUS!

He's

just

sooooo...

...little.

DOWNLOAD YOUR FREE
AUGMENTED REALITY app
Interactive app turns "It's Just So…" into a
pop-up book… includes narrated story,
music and games for all mobile devices.
Go to: PFVROOM

PlayingForward

www.playingforward.com
ItsJustSoBooks

ISBN-13: 978-0-9970851-2-9
[Juvenile Fiction - Picture Book - New Baby – ages 3-8]

Library of Congress Control Number: 2016919569
Faatz, Brenda & Trimarco, Peter
It's Just So…Little / written by Brenda Faatz / Peter Trimarco and illustrated by Peter Trimarco – 1st ed.
Summary: It's Just So… adventurous for a little girl named Lizzy as she faces challenges of growth and change. She and her faithful puppy adopt a frail little sapling tree, taking on the job of protecting and nurturing their new, well-rooted 'friend' throughout the seasons. In the meantime, Lizzy is outgrowing all of her favorite clothes and watching as Mom seems to be outgrowing her clothes as well. Lizzy's biggest change comes in welcoming the new baby as her family tree is growing too.

Printed in the USA by Worzalla, Stevens Point Wisconsin
Typography: Museo, Cooper, American Typewriter
The illustrations were done with pen & ink on bristol board, with backgrounds painted in acrylic on canvas.
Spot colors and additional finish work created in photoshop. Etcha-sketch was not used in any form, nor were any animals harmed in the creation of this book of fiction.
Lizzy Character ©2015 - 2017 Faatz & Trimarco